Unidade na Diversidade

Unity in Diversity: Portuguese

Melanie Lotfali

~ Credits ~

Autora & Ilustradora - Melanie Lotfali

Tradução - Nika & Shakib Shahidian

Livros nesta colecção

Os Tais de Deus

God's Tais

Atesa, Akala, Aleki, Zenha and Abel love their parents. One day they decide to make a present for their parents. They go to buy some cotton to make tais.

A Atesa, Akala, Aleki, Zenha e Abel adoram os seus pais. Um dia decidiram dar uma prenda aos seus pais. Por isso, foram comprar um pouco de algodão para fazer uns tais.

Atesa's favorite color is green. She makes a green tais. Akala likes yellow. She makes a yellow tais.

A cor favorita da Atesa é verde. Ela fez um tais verde. A Akala gosta de amarelo. Ela fez um tais amarelo.

OF COLOR.
LET'S ENJOY WITH THE COLOR INCREMENT OF
FLO

Aleki's favorite color is red. He uses red cotton to make a tais for his parents. Zenha thinks that pink is the most beautiful.

A cor favorita do Aleki é vermelho. Ele utilizou algodão vermelho para fazer um tais para dar aos seus pais. Zenha acha que cor-de-rosa é a cor mais bonita.

English	Português
Abel says that blue is the best. He makes a blue tais.	Abel diz que azul é a melhor cor. Ele fez um tais azul.

When they finish their tais the children go and play. They leave the scraps of cotton on the ground. Ameta walks past and finds the cotton left by the other children. She uses the cotton to make a tais.

Quando acabaram os seus tais, as crianças foram brincar. Eles deixaram os restos de algodão no chão. Ameta, que passava por ai, encontrou os restos de algodão deixados pelas outras crianças. Ela utilizou o algodão para fazer um tais.

Atesa's parents like
the green tais that
Atesa made
for them.

Os pais da Atesa
gostaram do tais
verde que ela lhes
ofereceu.

English

Akala, Aleki, Zenha and Abel's parents also like the yellow, red, pink and blue tais that their children made for them.

Português

Os pais de Akala, Aleki, Zenha e Abel também gostaram dos tais amarelo, vermelho, cor-de-rosa e azul que os seus filhos lhes ofereceram.

English

But Ameta's parents were the happiest of all because their tais was made of many different colors.

Português

Mas os pais da Ameta eram os mais felizes, porque o seu tais era feito de muitas cores diferentes.

The people of the
world are many
different colors.
Different colored
cotton makes a tais
more beautiful. And
different colored
people make our
world family more
beautiful.

As pessoas do
mundo são como as
diferentes cores. O
algodão de diferentes
cores torna o tais
mais bonito. E as
pessoas de
diferentes cores
tornam a nossa
família mundial mais
bonita.

The Earth is
but one country,
and mankind
its citizens.

~ Bahá'í Writings ~

A terra é um
só país e
a humanidade
seus cidadãos.

~ Escritos Bahá'ís ~

O Olho que Queira Viver Sozinho

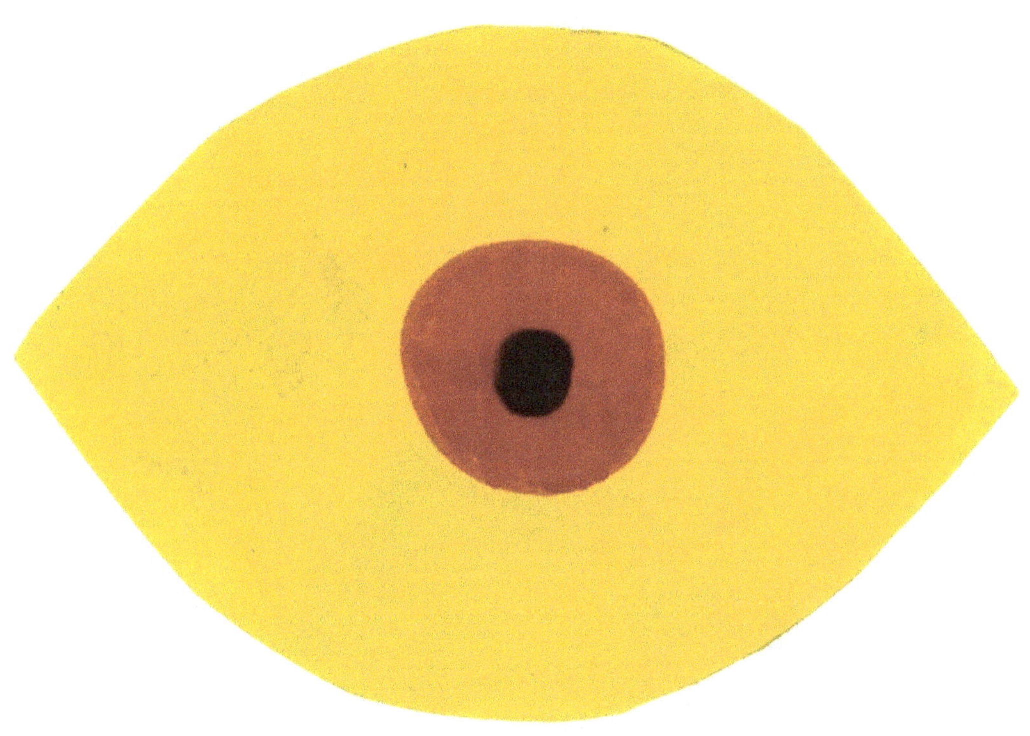

The Eye that Wanted to Live Alone

Once upon a time there lived a Body. This Body had all the things that bodies usually have, like two eyes, two hands, tummy, back, hair, ten fingers, and a bottom.

Era uma vez um Corpo que estava saudável. Este corpo tinha todas as coisas que os corpos normalmente têm: tinha dois olhos, duas mãos, uma barriga, costas, cabelo, dez dedos e um rabinho.

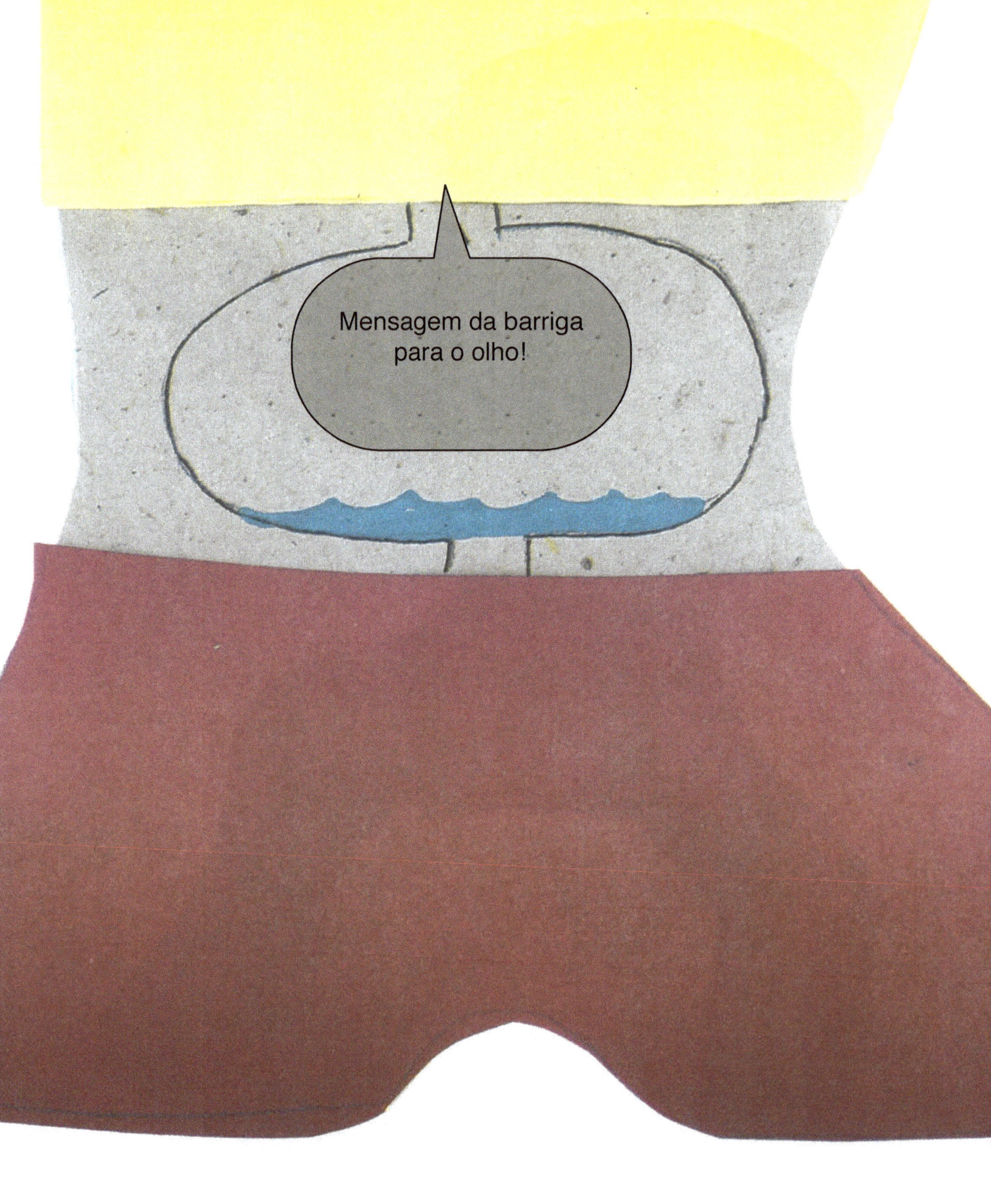

Mensagem da barriga
para o olho!

The parts of the Body were different and played different roles but they all worked together successfully.

For example, when Tummy felt empty, she told Eye to look for something to eat.

As partes do Corpo eram diferentes e desempenhavam funções diferentes, mas trabalhavam todos em conjunto.

Por exemplo, quando a barriga se sentia vazia, pedia ao Olho para procurar algo para comer.

Eye looked for food and then told Hand to take it. Hand took the food, Mouth opened and received the food. Teeth chewed the food and Tummy received the food. Tummy turned it into energy which it sent to Arms and Legs so that they could do their work. And so, all the parts of the body worked together in harmony.

O olho procurava comida e depois dizia à Mão para a apanhar. As mãos apanhavam a comida, a Boca abria e recebia a comida. Os dentes mastigavam a comida e a Barriga recebia a comida. A Barriga depois transformava a comida em energia que mandava para os Braços e as Pernas para poderem fazer o seu trabalho. Assim, todas as partes do corpo trabalhavam em harmonia como uma equipa.

<table>
<tr><td>

English

But, one day, Eye started to think that she was more important than the other body parts.

She thought: "If I don't look for food, Hand doesn't know where to get it. Then, Mouth doesn't know to open and Tummy stays empty. I am the most important!"

</td><td>

Português

Mas um dia, o Olho começou a pensar que era mais importante do que as outras partes do corpo.

Pensou para si: "Se eu não procurar comida, as Mãos não sabem onde está, e a Boca não se abre e a Barriga fica vazia. Eu sou o mais importante!"

</td></tr>
</table>

Eye ordered the other body parts to call her Queen Eye.

She told them that she was the most important and they should honor her. But the other body parts didn't agree.

They said to Eye: "No, we all need each other. We all help each other and depend on each other."

O olho mandou às outras partes do corpo para lhe chamarem de Rei Olho.

Disse-lhes que era o mais importante e que lhe deviam fazer as honras. Mas as outras partes do corpo não concordaram.

Disseram ao Olho: "Não, nós precisamos todos uns dos outros. Nós ajudamo-nos uns aos outros e dependemos uns dos outros."

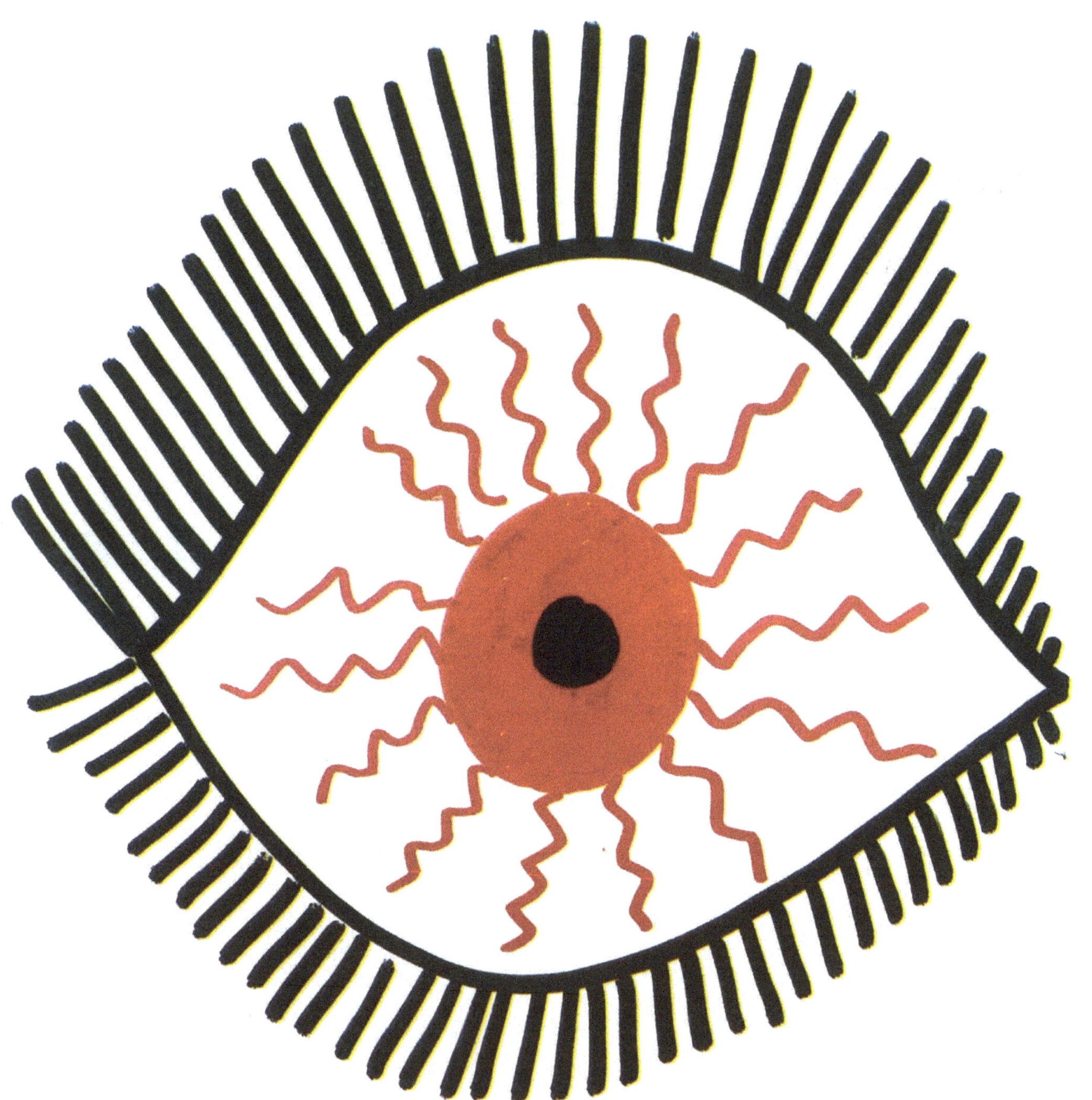

English

When Eye heard that they didn't accept that she was most important, she was angry!

She said: **"If you don't accept that I am queen, and if you don't honor me, I will not live with you!"**

Português

Quando o Olho descobriu que os outros não o aceitavam como sendo o mais importante, ficou muito zangado!

O olho disse: **"Se não me aceitarem como o vosso Rei e se não me prestarem honras, irei-vos abandonar!"**

English

Eye popped out of Face.
She went to live alone on
the table top.

Português

O Olho saltou para fora da
cara e foi viver sozinho em
cima da mesa.

The body parts felt very sad that Eye didn't want to live with them. A couple of hours later, Tummy felt empty. She sent a message to Eye's place, but there was no Eye.

So the message was sent directly to Hand. Hand received the message but didn't know what to do. He didn't know where to find food.

As restantes partes do corpo ficaram muito tristes pelo facto do Olho não querer viver com eles.

Passadas algumas horas, a Barriga sentiu-se vazia. Mandou uma mensagem para o lugar do Olho, mas o Olho não estava ali. Então a mensagem foi directamente para a Mão. A mão recebeu a mensagem, mas não sabia o que fazer. Não sabia onde encontrar comida.

Hand began to look for food by feeling. This took a long time but in the end he found a banana and gave it to Mouth. Mouth received it. Teeth chewed it. Tummy turned it into energy and sent it to Arms and Legs. Body suffered, but it didn't die.

A Mão começou a apalpar as coisas à procura de comida. Isso demorou muito tempo, mas no fim encontrou uma banana que deu à Boca. A Boca recebeu a banana. Os Dentes mastigaram-na. A Barriga transformou-a em energia e mandou-a para os braços e as pernas. O Corpo sofreu, mas não morreu.

Meanwhile Eye sat alone on the table top. She sat and thought about how she was more important than the other parts. But after some time she also began to lose energy. Alone she could not get food, chew it or turn it into energy.

Entretanto o Olho sentou-se sozinho em cima da mesa. Sentou-se e pensou sobre como era mais importante do que as outras partes. Mas depois de algum tempo, também começou a perder energia. Sozinho não podia arranjar comida, mastiga-la ou transformá-la em energia.

In the end she was about to die. She called the Body and said: "Help me please. I am about to die."

The Body said to Eye: "You are right. You can't live alone. We need your help and you also need us. Let's help each other." Hand picked up Eye and put her back in Face.

No fim estava quase a morrer. Chamou o Corpo e disse: "Por favor ajuda-me. Estou quase a morrer."

O Corpo respondeu: "Tens razão. Não consegues viver sozinho. Nós precisamos da tua ajuda e tu precisas da nossa. Vamo-nos ajudar uns aos outros." A Mão apanhou o Olho e colocou-o de novo na Cara.

Eye began to receive energy from the food that Tummy received from Hand and Mouth. Eye didn't die. She felt happy.

Eye said sorry to the other parts and said: "I made a mistake. You were right. We should all work together. We are all important, and we need unity to live well together."

O Olho começou a receber a energia da comida que a Barriga tinha recebido da Mão e da Boca. O Olho não morreu. Sentiu-se feliz.

O Olho pediu desculpas às restantes partes do Corpo e disse: "Cometi um erro. Vocês tinham razão. Devemos todos trabalhar em conjunto. Somos todos importantes e precisamos da unidade para viver bem uns com os outros."

Be ye as the fingers
of one hand,
the members
of one body.

~ Bahá'í Writings ~

Sede como os dedos
de uma só mão,
os membros
do mesmo corpo.

~ Escritos Bahá'ís ~

O Acorde Perfeito

A Perfect Chord

Indi-bird loved to sing.
She knew how to sing
one note. She sang it
beautifully and with all
her heart.

O pássaro Indy
adorava cantar. Ela só
sabia cantar uma única
nota. Ela cantava-a
lindamente e com todo
o seu coração.

English

One day Jarrah-bird came to visit. He also knew how to sing one note. They sang together.

Português

Um dia o pássaro Jarrah veio visitá-la. Ele também só sabia cantar uma única nota. Eles cantaram juntos.

Attracted by the sound, Tai-bird landed on the branch. He also knew how to sing just one note. It was different from the others. He added his note to the chord.

O pássaro Tai que passava por perto, ficou encantado com a música. Ele juntou-se aos outros dois. Ele também só sabia cantar uma única nota, que era diferente das outras. Ele juntou a sua nota à dos outros.

Marama-bird heard the beautiful harmony of the three different notes.

"I can sing a note too," she chirped. She joined the group.

O pássaro Marama ouviu o som maravilhoso das três notas.

Ele pensou "Eu também sei cantar uma nota". Por isso, juntou-se ao grupo.

Tama-bird flew in with a long loud "Cheeeeep Cheeeep". Joyfully he added his note to the music.

O pássaro Tama, com muita alegria, também se juntou aos outros, cantando a sua nota.

The harmony of the different notes was like a magnet for Mihi and Skye. They glided over to the branch.

They opened their beaks and sang their notes. Each bird's note was different from the others. Each note was beautiful. Together they made the perfect chord.

A harmonia das diferentes notas atraiu o Mihi e a Skye. Eles pousaram no ramo.

Eles abriram os seus bicos e cantaram as suas notas. A nota de cada pássaro era diferente das notas dos outros. Cada nota era bela. Juntos formaram o acorde perfeito.

The diversity in the human
family should be the cause
of love and harmony, as it is
in music where many
different notes blend
together in the making of
a perfect chord.

~ Bahá'í Writings ~

A diversidade na família
humana deve ser a causa
de amor e harmonia, tal
como acontece na música,
em que muitas notas
diferentes se juntam para
fazer um acorde perfeito.

~ Escritos Bahá'ís ~

Estrelas do Mesmo Céu

Stars of One Heaven

English

Clara was all alone. Clara was lonely. She looked up at the sky. She saw the sky was full of stars.

She turned to one and said: "You are so lucky. You have so many friends. I am all alone. I want a friend."

Português

A Clara estava sozinha. A Clara sentia-se sozinha. Ela olhou para o céu. O céu estava cheio de estrelas.

Ela virou-se para uma e disse: "Tens tanta sorte. Tens tantos amigos. Eu estou tão sozinha. Eu quero um amigo."

Star said: "Clara, why don't you ask God for a friend?"

So Clara prayed. She asked God to send her a friend.

When she opened her eyes she saw that God had sent her a friend.

"Oh no!" said Clara. "I want a friend just like me! He is different from me!"

A estrela respondeu: "Clara, porque é que não pedes a Deus para te dar um amigo?"

Por isso, a Clara orou. Pediu a Deus para lhe enviar um amigo.

Quando abriu os olhos, viu que Deus lhe tinha enviado um amigo.

"Oh não!" disse ela. "Eu queira um amigo igualzinho a mim! Este amigo é diferente de mim!"

Clara closed her eyes and prayed again. Then, she opened her eyes.

"Oh no!" sobbed Clara.

"I want a friend just like me! She is different from me!"

A Clara fechou os seus olhos e orou de novo. Depois abriu os seus olhos.

"Oh não!" disse ela.

"Eu quero uma amiga igualzinha a mim! Esta amiga é diferente de mim!"

English

Clara closed her eyes and prayed again. Then, she opened her eyes.

"Oh no!" cried Clara. "I want a friend just LIKE ME! She is DIFFERENT from me!"

Clara threw herself on the grass. She cried and cried. The new friends wandered away.

Português

A Clara fechou os seus olhos e orou de novo. Depois abriu os seus olhos.

"Oh não!" disse ela. "Eu quero uma amiga IGUALZINHA a mim! Esta amiga é DIFERENTE de mim!"

A Clara atirou-se para o chão e chorou e chorou. Os novos amigos foram-se embora.

That night she turned to Star. "Why does God keep sending me the wrong thing?" she asked.

Star said to Clara: "When you look up to the sky, what do you see?"

Nessa noite, ela olhou para as estrelas. "Porque é que Deus está-me sempre a mandar a pessoa errada?" perguntou ela.

A estrela respondeu: "Quando olhas para o céu, o que é que vês?"

English

Clara said: "I see beautiful stars shining brightly."

Star said: "That's right. We are all different shapes, colors, and sizes. But when you look up you see our unity. You see we are all stars."

Português

A Clara disse: "Vejo lindas estrelas a brilhar."

A estrela respondeu: "É verdade. Nós temos todos cores, formas e tamanhos diferentes. Mas quando olhas para cima vês a nossa unidade. Vês que somos todas estrelas."

"When I look down," said Star, "I see beautiful human beings. It doesn't matter that you are different shapes, colors, and sizes. You are all human beings."

"Oh yes!" laughed Clara.

"Now, where did they go, those friends just like me?"

"Quando olho para baixo", disse a estrela, "vejo seres humanos lindos. Não interessa que vocês tenham formas, cores e tamanhos diferentes. São todos seres humanos."

"Oh sim!" riu a Clara.

"Onde é que foram esses amigos meus, esses amigos parecidos comigo?"

...love will make

them all the stars

of one heaven.

~ Bahá'í Writings ~

...amor fará de todos os homens estrelas do mesmo céu.

~ Escritos Bahá'ís ~

Frutos de Uma Só Árvore

The Fruit of One Tree

When I get up I see our
fruit bowl. It is full of
ripe yellow bananas.
Today I want to eat
bananas for breakfast,
lunch, and dinner. I
peel a banana and
take a big bite.

Quando me levanto
vejo o nosso cesto de
frutas. Está cheio de
bananas amarelas e
maduras. Hoje quero
comer bananas ao
pequeno-almoço,
almoço e jantar.
Descasco uma banana
e dou uma grande
dentada.

Then I see Maria
selling mangos. I
remember how sweet
and slimy they are.
Maria sells me
some mangos.

Depois vejo a Maria
que está a vender
mangas. Lembro-me do
seu sabor delicioso.
Compro algumas
mangas à Maria.

English

When I go to the tap to wash the mango juice from my chin, I see our paw paw tree. Paw paw with lime juice. My favourite!

Português

Quando vou até à torneira lavar a cara dos restos da manga, vejo a nossa árvore de papaia. Hum!!! Papaia com sumo de lima. Que maravilha! O meu preferido!

English

Even with my belly full of paw paw, the orange tree catches my eye. I pull an orange off the branch. I peel it and break the orange ball into pieces. I put them in my mouth one by one.

Português

Mesmo com o estômago cheio de papaia, a laranjeira chama-me a atenção. Apanho uma laranja. Descasco-a e como-a gomo a gomo.

I start to think:
Bananas are yummy.
Mangos are sweet.
Paw paws are
delicious. Oranges
are tasty.

Começo a pensar:
As bananas são
deliciosas. As mangas
são doces. As Papaias
são fantásticas. As
laranjas são
saborosas.

What if we put them together? What if we ate them mixed together? That would be the best of all.

E se as juntássemos todas? E se as comêssemos todas juntas? Seria a melhor coisa a fazer.

Yummy, sweet,
delicious, tasty
Fruit Salad!

Uma salada de fruta
deliciosa, doce,
fantástica e saborosa!

O people of the world,
ye are all the fruit of
one tree and the leaves
of one branch.

~ Bahá'í Writings ~

Ó povo do mundo:
Sois os frutos de uma
só árvore e as folhas
do mesmo ramo.

~ Escritos Bahá'ís ~

Fellowship Farm

Volume 1: BOOKS 1-3

Leezah, Skye-Maree and Olingah Fitzgerald live with their parents on Fellowship Farm. In the first book of the Fellowship Farm series, you will meet the children and learn about their daily activities on the farm. There is a lot to be done each day: pillow fights, morning prayers, pig feeding and school bus riding. They help their dad feed the cows, add stickers to their virtues poster and learn to deal with bullies.

Then you will join the Fitzgerald children on their many adventures with puppies, snake bites, treasure hunts, bonfires, camping by the sea, and tree houses. And as they go they sometimes practice their virtues, and sometimes forget…

Suitable for independent readers aged 8-12 years; parent-read from six years. Order online from print-on-demand services, and digitally from the iBookstore or Kindle.

Fellowship Farm

Volume 2: BOOKS 4-6

Leezah, Skye-Maree and Olingah Fitzgerald live with their parents on Fellowship Farm. In the first volume of the Fellowship Farm series, you met the children and learned about their daily activities on the farm.

In this the second volume the Fitzgerald children are visited by their cousins, Nick and Anisa. Together they travel by horse and cart to the market, attend the 19 Day Feast, go camping, find a pirate map and treasure, as well as experience the intensity of crisis and victory when Olingah's life is put in serious danger.

Suitable for independent readers aged 8-12 years; parent-read from six years. Order online from print-on-demand services, and digitally from the iBookstore or Kindle.

Fellowship Farm

Volume 3: BOOKS 7-9

In this, the third volume of stories about Leezah, Skye-Maree and Olingah Fitzgerald who live with their parents on Fellowship Farm, the children set out with joy to go blackberry picking.

But an unexpected turn of events at the river makes them fear for the lives of their puppies. Ayyám-i-Há follows with serving, teaching, gifts, treasure-hunts as well as the challenge of bullying for Skye-Maree. After Ayyám-i-Há comes an opportunity to visit their eccentric Uncle Jack who takes them to the chocolate factory, aquatic centre and gives them many other treats both spiritual and edible!

Suitable for independent readers aged 8-12 years; parent-read from six years. Order online from print-on-demand services, and digitally from the iBookstore or Kindle.

Fellowship Farm

Volume 4: BOOKS 10-12

In the fourth volume of stories about Leezah, Skye-Maree and Olingah Fitzgerald of Fellowship Farm they prepare for the annual Naw Ruz Mahta River Boat Race. There are some unexpected hitches.

Skye-Maree and Olingah learn about loyalty and sacrifice as they work out how to respond to the challenges they face. Soon after Naw Ruz winter sets in and the family rug up and head for the ski slopes.

Along the way they experience the life-threatening danger of losing unity, the challenge of learning to ski, the power of prayer, and patience in the face of frustration. They meet funny Magic, the back to front panda, and suffer some bruises. Their patience is well rewarded when their parents announce that a dear wish of the children is to be fulfilled.

Suitable for independent readers aged 8-12 years; parent-read from six years. Order online from print-on-demand services, and digitally from the iBookstore or Kindle.

Unity in Diversity

This brightly illustrated picture book contains five simple stories for young readers. They foster an understanding of the oneness of the human race and celebrate its diversity within that unity.

Likening the human race to various colored cotton in a woven cloth, various fruits on the tree of life, stars in the heavens, members of one body, and different notes in one perfect chord, the stories use the concrete to teach the abstract.

Young readers will enjoy the bright colors and simple text as they develop their understanding of the unity and diversity of the human race.

Ideal for children aged 4-8 years.
Order online from print-on-demand services, and digitally from the iBookstore. Translated into French, Portuguese, Romanian, Tetum, and Mongolian.

The Big Story

The Big Story explains the way in which the divinely ordained and guided process that has brought human beings into existence has taken place gradually over time and space. It shows that the concepts of evolution and creation are not mutually exclusive.

Science and religion are shown to be two windows on one reality, two knowledge systems that when properly understood, function as one cohesive whole.

This book is most suitable for readers 14 years and older. Younger readers will enjoy the bright and informative illustrations but will require support to understand the text.

Suitable for independent readers aged 14+ years; with assistance from 12+. Order online from print-on-demand services, and digitally from the iBookstore.

Dr Melanie Lotfali

Author of The Fitzgeralds of Fellowship Farm series and Unity in Diversity series.

Melanie Lotfali PhD is a graduate of the Australian College of Journalism in Professional Writing for Children. She is the author of eighteen books of fiction and non-fiction for children and the illustrator of five.

Melanie has taught spiritual education classes for children for the past twenty years in five countries and is currently an active animator and trainer of animators for the Junior Youth Spiritual Empowerment Program. She is a qualified counselor and classroom teacher, and for the past six years has facilitated violence prevention and respectful relationships programs in high schools.

Much of her childhood was spent on the farms, beaches and mountains of Tasmania, where the Fellowship Farm series is set. As an adult she spent four years in Siberia and four years in East Timor as a pioneer.

She currently lives in Lismore, Australia, with her family.

Michael Cohen

Author of The Big Story and publisher of all Michelangela books.

Michael Cohen graduated as a Computer Systems Engineer in 1990 and worked for many years in software design and informations systems. He changed careers in 2008 to become a Registered Nurse working in the area of Mental Health and Alcohol & Other Drugs.

Michael has been a keen participant in and advocate of the programs offered by **The Foundation for the Application and Teaching of the Sciences** (FUNDAEC) and **Institute for Studies in Global Prosperity** (ISGP). He strives to contribute to processes and discourses leading to the progress of humankind toward a world society characterized by unity, justice and equity. A fundamental premise of Michael's worldview is that true science and true religion are necessarily in harmony, indeed are two windows on one reality. His writing seeks to promote understanding of this liberating concept and to contribute to a civilization that is ever advancing materially and spiritually.

He currently lives in Lismore, Australia, with his family.

Michelangela

website - www.michelangela.com.au
email - info@michelangela.com.au

To receive Michelangela's occasional
product announcements
please visit our website and
enter your email address and name
via the subscribe button

Warm Regards,
Melanie & Michael of Michelangela.